A Kiss Like This

Mary Murphy

kiss

kiss

A giraffe kiss
is gentle and
tall...

A mouse
kiss
is
quick

and
small...

like
this!

A
fish kiss
is fizzy and

bubbly . . .

like
this!

A bee kiss is fuzzy

and buzzy...

like this!

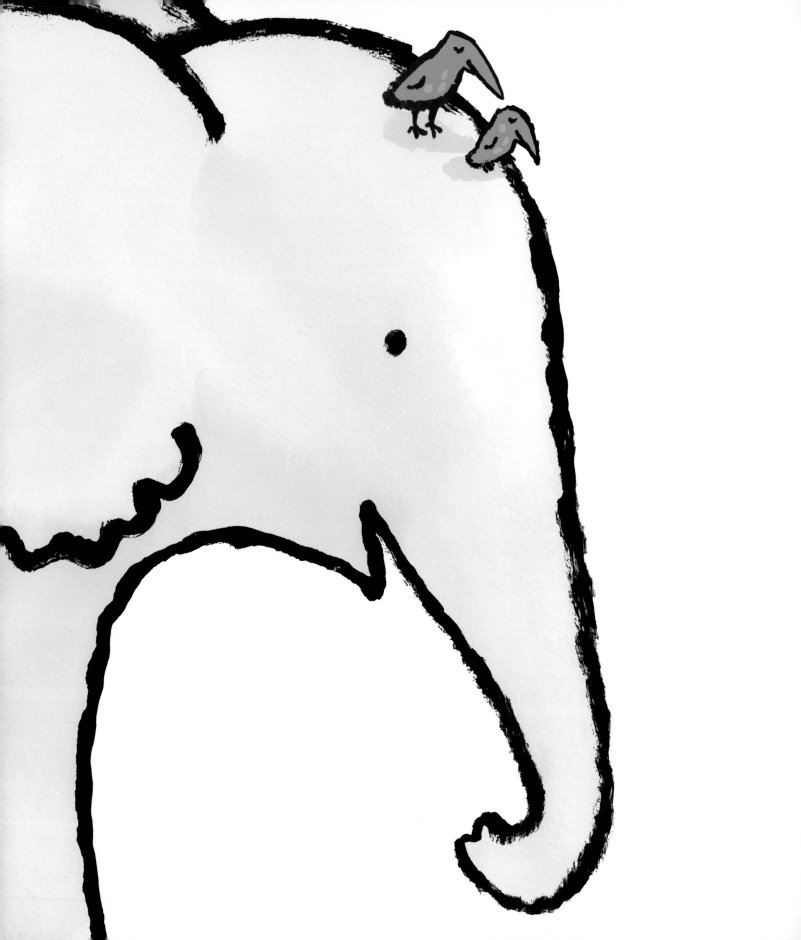

An
elephant
kiss is
long and
toot-tooty...

like
this!

kiss

TOOTY

An owl kiss is
tu-wit
tu-wooty . . .

like this!

Your kiss!